Sea Serpents Don't Juggle Water Balloons

Story Link®
Program

There are more books about the Bailey School kids!
Have you read these adventures?

#1 Vampires Don't Wear Polka Dots
#2 Werewolves Don't Go to Summer Camp
#3 Santa Claus Doesn't Mop Floors
#4 Leprechauns Don't Play Basketball
#5 Ghosts Don't Eat Potato Chips
#6 Frankenstein Doesn't Plant Petunias
#7 Aliens Don't Wear Braces
#8 Genies Don't Ride Bicycles
#9 Pirates Don't Wear Pink Sunglasses
#10 Witches Don't Do Backflips
#11 Skeletons Don't Play Tubas
#12 Cupid Doesn't Flip Hamburgers
#13 Gremlins Don't Chew Bubble Gum
#14 Monsters Don't Scuba Dive
#15 Zombies Don't Play Soccer
#16 Dracula Doesn't Drink Lemonade
#17 Elves Don't Wear Hard Hats
#18 Martians Don't Take Temperatures
#19 Gargoyles Don't Drive School Buses
#20 Wizards Don't Need Computers
#21 Mummies Don't Coach Softball
#22 Cyclops Doesn't Roller-skate
#23 Angels Don't Know Karate
#24 Dragons Don't Cook Pizza
#25 Bigfoot Doesn't Square Dance
#26 Mermaids Don't Run Track
#27 Bogeymen Don't Play Football
#28 Unicorns Don't Give Sleigh Rides
#29 Knights Don't Teach Piano
#30 Hercules Doesn't Pull Teeth
#31 Ghouls Don't Scoop Ice Cream
#32 Phantoms Don't Drive Sports Cars
#33 Giants Don't Go Snowboarding
#34 Frankenstein Doesn't Slam Hockey Pucks
#35 Trolls Don't Ride Roller Coasters
#36 Wolfmen Don't Hula Dance
#37 Goblins Don't Play Video Games
#38 Ninjas Don't Bake Pumpkin Pies
#39 Dracula Doesn't Rock and Roll
#40 Sea Monsters Don't Ride Motorcycles
#41 The Bride of Frankenstein Doesn't Bake Cookies
#42 Robots Don't Catch Chicken Pox
#43 Vikings Don't Wear Wrestling Belts
#44 Ghosts Don't Ride Wild Horses
#45 Wizards Don't Wear Graduation Gowns
The Bailey School Kids Joke Book
Super Special #1: Mrs. Jeepers Is Missing!
Super Special #2: Mrs. Jeepers' Batty Vacation
Super Special #3: Mrs. Jeepers' Secret Cave
Super Special #4: Mrs. Jeepers in Outer Space
Super Special #5: Mrs. Jeepers' Monster Class Trip
Super Special #6: Mrs. Jeepers on Vampire Island
Holiday Special: Swamp Monsters Don't Chase Wild Turkeys

Sea Serpents Don't Juggle Water Balloons

by Debbie Dadey
and
Marcia Thornton Jones

illustrated by John Steven Gurney

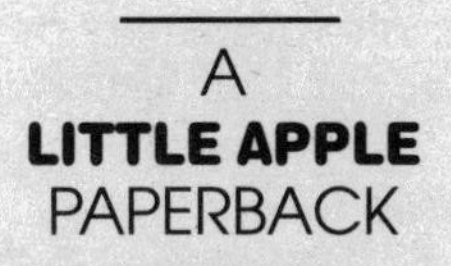

SCHOLASTIC INC.
New York Toronto London Auckland Sydney
Mexico City New Delhi Hong Kong Buenos Aires

For Brantley
and
Hannah Rosenfeld
— MTJ

To Justin, Christina, and Sean Pellman —
great neighbors.
— DD

ISBN 0-439-36805-7

12 11 10 9 8 7 6 5 4 3 2 3 4 5 6 7/0

Printed in the U.S.A. 40
First Scholastic printing, January 2002

Contents

1

Summer Festival

"Bombs away!" Eddie shouted just as a water balloon smashed into Liza's back. She was wet from the tip of her blond ponytail all the way down to her sneakers, and she was not very happy about it.

"You did that on purpose," she snapped at Eddie.

"It's only water," Eddie said. "You're not the Wicked Witch of the West — you won't melt."

Liza and Eddie were in Bailey City Park near the pool. It was Summer Festival week and the park was full of booths with fun events. Liza and Eddie had been trying to learn how to juggle. They were supposed to start by juggling tennis balls, but Eddie had skipped that part and went for the water balloons instead. But Eddie

wasn't trying to juggle them. He was lobbing them at nearby kids.

"I'll get you for that," Liza warned him.

"Yeah?" Eddie asked with a grin. "You and what army?"

"Just wait," Liza told him. "You'll be sorry!"

Liza stomped off across Bailey City Park, away from Eddie. She wasn't gone long. She came back with reinforcements, her good friends Howie and Melody.

When Eddie saw them, he pushed his ball cap down tight on his red hair and grabbed two water balloons. He wasn't fast enough.

"Look out!" Howie said and blasted a water balloon at Eddie. Melody laughed as she tossed two balloons at Eddie's chest.

"Give up?" Liza said, dropping a water balloon on Eddie's head.

"Never!" Eddie yelled. "I'm no quitter!" He threw another balloon in their direction, but he missed and it hit a kid named

Huey who happened to be walking by. Before long, every kid in the park was tossing water balloons, but nobody was wetter than Eddie.

Liza giggled. "Eddie, you look like a sea serpent."

"No, he doesn't," Huey said as he squeezed water out of his shirt. "Sea serpents are long and skinny."

"They're slimy and slithery," a girl named Jane added.

"Sea serpents are cold-blooded and have a snake's tongue," Melody said as she wrung water from one of her braids. Then she smiled. "Hey, now that you mention it, Eddie *does* look like a big snake."

Eddie stuck out his tongue at Melody.

"See," she said with a giggle, "he even flicks his tongue like a serpent."

"No," the boy named Huey said. "Eddie doesn't look like a sea serpent, but *that* guy sure does."

2

The Perfect SSSpot

A tall, skinny man dressed in a bright green wet suit climbed out of the pool. He was so thin they could see the bumps of his spine through his shiny suit. The man had slicked-back hair and huge ears that reminded Melody of a fish's gills because they stuck straight out from his head. Melody blinked. She was sure she saw his ears wiggle as he climbed out of the pool.

The man smiled at a group of kids still trying to juggle. "I'll ssshow you how to do that," he said.

"Listen to him," Eddie said. "He sounds like a steam engine."

"It's not nice to make fun of people," Liza said, giving Eddie a light jab in his side. "He can't help the way he talks."

The tall man wound around a group of sunbathers to the juggling booth, leaving behind a crooked trail of water. "Juggling is quite sssimple," he told them. "I will teach you. It only takesss concentration."

"Eddie may as well give up right now," Melody said with a giggle. "He's not known for using his brain."

"I'll never give up," Eddie said.

"Quitters never succeed," Howie added. "I bet we could learn to juggle if we practiced enough."

The stranger smiled at Howie. "Practice," he said, "isss exactly what it takesss." He began juggling, tossing water balloons rhythmically into the air. A group of kids crowded around to watch.

The swimmer's body swayed back and forth as if he were listening to distant music. The tip of his tongue darted out the corner of his mouth. He gazed at a faraway tree, almost as if he were hypnotized.

Eddie watched for a full twenty-four seconds. "I can do it, I can do it," Eddie muttered in time with the man's juggling. Then, before his friends could stop him, Eddie pushed to the front of the crowd. "LET ME TRY!" he hollered.

The man jumped back and blinked three times as if he'd forgotten the kids were there. *SPLAT. SPLAT. SPLAT.* All three balloons burst on the ground.

"Gee," Eddie said. "I didn't mean to scare you."

The man glared down at Eddie for a moment. The sun caught the green of the man's eyes, turning the pupils to narrow slits. Then, slowly, he smiled. "You ssstartled me. That'sss all."

"Eddie tends to have that effect on most grown-ups," Liza said.

Eddie frowned at Liza. Then he turned back to the stranger. "How did you learn to juggle like that? Can you teach me?"

"Asss your friend mentioned, juggling

takesss practice. I have been practicing for a long, long time. In fact," he told them, "thisss isss my booth. I travel with the organizersss of the SSSummer Fesstival."

"I bet working for the Summer Festival is fun," Huey said.

Eddie nodded. "That would be the perfect job for me. Just think about it. No reading. No math. No homework. Just fun, fun, fun!"

The man didn't look as happy as Eddie thought he should. Instead, the man shook his head and sighed. "Flitting from one place to another isss very tiring. In fact, I am looking for a cozy place to sssettle; a nice, quiet town would be the perfect ssspot for me."

Melody giggled. "That sounds like Bailey City," she said, "if it wasn't for Eddie."

Howie nodded. "Eddie is the noisiest kid in Bailey City."

"Ask any teacher," Liza added.

Eddie grinned. He was proud of how

loud he could be. To prove it, he puffed out his chest and did an Ape Man yodel.

"Now, teach me to juggle," Eddie said as soon as he was finished yelling. "Please, please?"

The man eyed Eddie with his green eyes. "Perhapsss if I ssstay in Bailey City I could teach you," he said. "But right now the sssun is heating my ssskin. It'sss time for a cool dip in the pool."

He nodded good-bye to the kids, wound

his way back to the pool, and slipped into the water. He dove deep and swam along the bottom of the pool until he reached the other side.

Melody watched as the stranger rose for a breath before diving underwater again. His back arched briefly above the surface, and she was able to see every bump along his spine. The way he swam reminded her of something, but she just couldn't remember what it was.

Melody was so busy watching the man swim she didn't see Eddie's water balloon — until it was too late. *SPLAT!*

3

Far from Fun

The next day, Eddie found Melody, Liza, and Howie at the park trying out the Hula-Hoops since the juggling booth was closed. Melody tossed a green hoop over Eddie's head. "I bet you can't do this," she said. Then she sent her purple hoop zooming around her waist.

Eddie's hoop clattered to the ground around his feet. He didn't even try to spin it around.

Liza held a red Hula-Hoop in her hand. Hula-Hoops made her dizzy so she wasn't able to get hers going. "What's wrong with you?" she asked Eddie.

Eddie let out such a big gush of air he looked like a balloon that had just popped. "It isn't fair," he moaned. "After all, it is summer."

TAKE ONE FOR A SPIN!
HULA-HOOP!

"What's wrong with summer?" Howie asked, spinning a blue hoop around his arm so fast it became a blur.

"I thought summer was your favorite season," Melody added, her purple hoop spinning around and around.

Eddie kicked his Hula-Hoop out of the way and plopped down on the ground, resting his chin in his hands.

"Why are you upset?" Liza asked Eddie. She sat down on the ground next to him.

"It's my grandmother," Eddie complained. "She's making me go to a math tutor. She said I have to make up for all the assignments I didn't do during the school year. It just isn't fair. I shouldn't have to be cooped up all summer with a teacher who thinks multiplication tables are the most exciting thing to happen in this world."

"That is awful," Melody said, laying her hoop on the ground. She sat down next to Eddie and Liza. "Summer is for relaxing."

Howie joined his friends. "Anytime is learning time, and your grandmother is right. You didn't even try to do some of those assignments during the regular school year. Now you have to catch up. Besides, math can be fun."

Eddie tossed a Hula-Hoop over Howie's head. "I didn't like math during the year. I know I won't like math during the summer."

"Yesterday you told us you weren't a quitter," Liza reminded him. "You can't quit on math."

"Maybe it won't be so bad," Melody told Eddie.

"It's worse than bad," Eddie said sadly, "because I have to start tutoring today. I can't even stay for the Summer Festival."

Liza tried to cheer up Eddie. "We'll go with you to your tutor's house," she said.

"We will?" Melody asked, looking around at all the neat things happening in the park.

"Of course we will," Liza said. "Friends stick together and we're your friends."

"Liza is right," Howie said. "We'll get our bikes and meet back here. We'll make it fun!"

"Okay," Eddie grumbled, "but I guarantee that this math tutor is going to be far from fun!"

4

Seaside Graveyard

"This is it," Eddie said, looking at the address written on the palm of his hand. The kids had ridden their bikes along the road that snaked around Swamp Dread. They parked their bikes under a shade tree.

"It doesn't look that bad," Melody said doubtfully.

"Not if you think the lost city of Atlantis is paradise," Eddie muttered.

The tutor's house wasn't a house at all. It was a broken-down camper parked near the trail that led straight down to Viper Pond. The camper was blue with green lines in the shape of waves painted on the side. A nearby wading pool was surrounded by seashells, and an old row-

S
E
W
N

boat was tipped on its side near the back of the camper. A wind-worn picnic table sat nearby.

"It looks like a seaside graveyard," Howie said.

"That's exactly what it is," Eddie said. "A graveyard for my summer fun."

"Tutoring won't be that bad," Howie said, patting Eddie on the back.

"You haven't even tried it yet," Melody added. "You might find you like learning."

"It will never happen," Eddie said with a sigh.

The kids walked up the sandy pathway to the camper's door. Eddie lifted his face to the sun and shouted, "I'm HEEEERRRRRREEE!" He pounded on the door just in case the tutor hadn't heard him. But he didn't knock once. He knocked five times. On the fifth knock, the door broke free from its latch and slowly squeaked open. No one was there.

Eddie was ready to step inside when the kids heard a big splash coming from Viper Pond.

"It sounds like your tutor has gone for a swim," Melody said.

"Maybe I'll get to swim instead of doing three-digit subtraction," Eddie said hopefully.

"Don't say that!" Liza said. "Everyone knows that Viper Pond is full of snakes."

Howie put his hand on Liza's arm. "It's not true," he said. "The pond isn't full of poisonous snakes. That's only a legend." Howie liked science and he was always doing research about animals. He even kept a notebook about the plants and animals he'd seen living in Bailey City.

"Do you mean to tell me there are *no* snakes in this pond?" Liza asked.

"Well," Howie said slowly, "there may be a little snake here or there."

Liza yelped and hopped up on the nearby picnic table. "Somebody has to tell Eddie's tutor that it's not safe to swim in that pond," she said, "but it's not going to be me."

"I'd tell — if I could find the tutor!" Eddie said. Eddie didn't like wasting precious summer minutes looking for a teacher. "Maybe we should leave."

"Or," Howie said, "we could hike down to the pond and see if we can spot your tutor."

"Howie's right," Melody said. "We'll come with you."

"We will?" Liza squeaked from her perch on the picnic table.

Melody nodded and held out her hand to help Liza down. "There is nothing to worry about," Melody assured Liza. "The only snakes around here are teeny-tiny, and they are more afraid of us than we are of them."

Liza looked around before gingerly stepping from the table to the bench and then to the ground.

“Everything will be okay,” Howie added.

“If everything was okay, I wouldn’t have to spend my summer with a tutor,” Eddie grumbled, but secretly he was very glad that his friends were staying.

5

Viper Pond

"It's this way," Howie told his friends. They walked along a path made of crushed seashells. Branches from weeping willow trees hung over the pathway and the kids had to push them aside to squeeze through.

"This place gives me the creeps," Liza complained.

"Why would anyone want to live here?" Melody whispered.

Eddie didn't whisper. He shouted. "Why would anyone want to study math?" Then, because he was mad, he yelled, "Hello! I'm here to be tutored!"

Quiet. Except for the buzz of the bugs in the trees, the kids heard nothing.

"Hello. Hello. HELLO!" Eddie screamed.

He stomped his foot with each word. Still, no one answered.

"Listen," Howie said. "I hear more splashing."

Liza couldn't keep her eyes off the ground. "Are you sure there aren't any giant snakes living in Viper Pond?"

"Positive," Howie said, but Liza still watched the trail for wiggling creatures.

"Come on," Eddie snapped. "The pond must be this way."

The kids stepped around a big boulder that jutted out over the trail. Liza looked at the boulder carefully. She had heard that snakes liked to hide near big rocks.

"Finally," Melody said. "We've found Viper Pond."

The kids stared at the pond. A thick coat of green slime covered the water. Tiny bugs skimmed the pond's surface. Here and there, a big log jutted up out of the slime.

"This place stinks," Liza said, holding her nose.

"Come on," Eddie grumbled, turning to leave. "There's no one here."

"Wait," Howie said, putting a hand on Eddie's arm. "Look."

In the middle of the pond, a huge splash rippled the green water. A strange shape appeared at the surface.

Eddie rubbed his eyes. "That's the weirdest thing I've ever seen."

Liza gulped. She didn't know what it was, but she definitely didn't like it.

Whatever it was moved toward the kids, the water parting as the creature glided closer and closer.

"It's coming to get us," Melody gasped.

"It's a sea serpent!" Liza screamed.

6

Seamus

A wet head appeared out of the slime. The kids stared in shock as a familiar face with big ears skimmed toward them.

"Hey," Melody said. "That's the juggler from the park."

The man nodded his slick head as he slowly climbed up on the shore. Today, he wore a bright orange wet suit. "Hello, my name is SSSeamus SSSandborn, but you can call me SSSeamus." He held out a dripping hand and shook each of their hands.

"Hello," Liza said, staring at green slime clinging to the man's wet suit. "I'm Liza, and this is Melody, Howie, and Eddie."

"Aren't you worried about snakes being in that pond?" Liza asked.

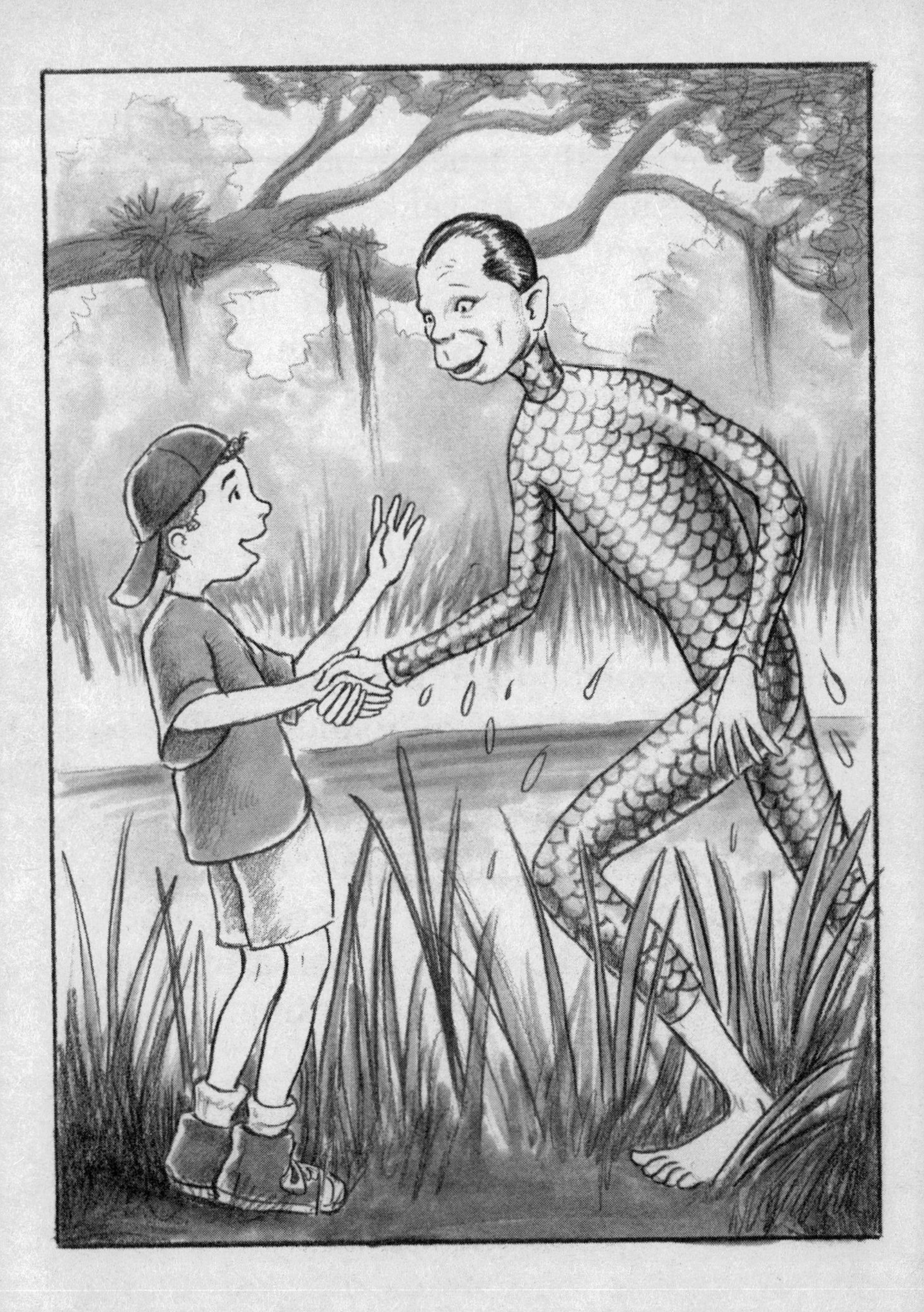

The man tilted his head back and chuckled softly. "I never have to worry about sssnakes," he said.

"Well, you need to worry about me," Eddie said, interrupting the man. "I'm the one you're supposed to tutor. But I'd much rather go swimming in the pond, especially if there are no snakes."

"I never sssaid there were no sssnakes," Seamus whispered.

Eddie didn't hear him. "Can I swim instead of adding numbers? Can I? Please?" Eddie hopped up and down and begged. Dust poofed out from around his sneakers with every jump.

Seamus put a damp hand on Eddie's shoulder to stop him from hopping up and down. "I'm afraid your grandmother wouldn't be happy if we took a dip," he said. "I'm ready to begin working. Follow me, pleassse."

Water and slime dripped from Seamus' suit, leaving a zigzagging trail back toward the camper. Melody couldn't help noticing how thin the man was.

"Eddie and I will work at the picnic table," Seamus told them when they reached the camper.

"I've never met a teacher who lived in a camper before," Eddie blurted.

Seamus smiled at Eddie. "Thisss isss only temporary. Asss sssoon asss I find a nice, quiet ssspot, I intend to ssstay put. I will carve out a more permanent den then."

"Do you think you'll stay in Bailey City?" Liza asked politely.

Seamus glanced around at the trees and then at the kids until his green eyes rested on Eddie. "SSSo far it'sss perfect, except for one little problem that I mussst take care of before deciding. Now, Eddie and I need to work. The ressst of you are welcome to wait in the camper. But you mussst be quiet," he warned them. "Very quiet."

Melody, Liza, and Howie climbed three

short steps to the camper door and went inside. “This is so strange,” Melody whispered as soon as the door clicked

shut behind them. The kids were surrounded by items from the sea: huge shells, seaweed, stuffed sharks, empty clamshells, pictures of dolphins, and large aquariums full of colorful fish.

“It looks like a scuba diver’s dream,” Liza admitted.

“Or,” Howie said softly, “a fisherman’s nightmare.”

7

No Ordinary Tutor

The walls of the tiny trailer were painted sea-foam green, the ceiling was blue, and the room was lined with aquariums. The kids slowly walked around, looking at the unusual creatures swimming behind the glass. "I've never seen so many fish in my life," Liza said.

"A normal person wouldn't need this many fish," Howie said.

Melody's eyes were big as she watched a fish dart back and forth in the aquarium. "I don't think Seamus is an ordinary person," she said slowly. "In fact, I don't think Seamus is a person at all!"

Liza looked at Melody. "What are you talking about? Just because someone collects fish, it doesn't mean he's a monster."

"We have to check on Eddie," Melody said suddenly. "Before it's too late."

"We just saw Eddie," Howie said. "He's fine. Besides, I can hear him from here."

It was true. Through the thin walls of the camper, the kids heard Eddie reciting math facts. Only Eddie didn't say them nicely. He shouted them. And with each answer, Eddie pounded the table so hard that the water in the aquariums shook.

"We have to do something. Fast. Seamus isn't an ordinary tutor," Melody said.

Liza nodded. "He isn't ordinary. After all, he can juggle. Most teachers can't juggle at all. Once, I saw a teacher try to hang on to four apples I'd given her and she dropped every one of them."

"Teachers can juggle if they keep trying. I'm going to practice with tennis balls tonight," Howie said. "I can show Seamus before the festival leaves town if I get good enough."

Melody stomped her foot, rattling a pile of seashells. "Stop talking about juggling," she snapped. "This is serious. We have to get Eddie away from Seamus."

"Why?" Liza said. "Don't you want Eddie to get better at math?"

"I want Eddie to stay safe, and he can't stay safe with a sea serpent around." Howie and Liza looked at all the aquariums. There wasn't a single sea serpent anywhere in the tanks.

Liza put her hand on Melody's shoulder. "I think you should sit down and rest. Maybe that smell from the pond got you mixed up."

"I can't sit down. Don't you guys understand? Seamus Sandborn is a sea serpent!"

8

Gone

Melody didn't wait for her friends. She flung open the camper door and jumped down the three steps.

Howie looked at Liza. "We have to stop Melody," he said. "I think she's gone nuts."

Howie and Liza took off after Melody. They almost crashed into her. She stood perfectly still, staring at the empty picnic table.

"He's gone!" Melody gasped. "We're too late."

"Where did they go?" Liza asked.

Howie looked around the yard. "They have to be around here somewhere."

Just then, they heard something. Something they never expected to hear. Eddie was laughing. "It sounds like they're down at the pond," Howie said.

"Oh, dear," Melody cried. "This is horrible. It's terrible. We have to save Eddie from being dragged into the slimy water by Seamus. If Eddie disappears into Viper Pond, we might never see him again."

Melody scrambled down the path and around the boulder. Howie and Liza dashed after her. They found Seamus and Eddie at the water's edge.

"Stop!" Melody screamed at Seamus as she rushed up and grabbed Eddie. "You can't have him!"

"We are almossst finished," Seamus told Melody. "He'll be ready in jussst a minute."

Eddie frowned at Melody and pulled his arm free from her grasp. "What is wrong with you? Seamus was showing me how to use math to find out the water temperature in different parts of the pond. It's the kind of thing scuba divers need to know. If I learn all this stuff,

maybe someday I can dive to the bottom of the ocean."

"That's really nice," Melody said, "but your grandmother needs you at home right away. She needs help . . ."

". . . Eating cookies," Liza added, saying the first thing that popped into her mind.

Melody glared at Liza before grabbing Eddie's arm. "Come on. We don't want those cookies to go to waste."

The kids pulled Eddie down the path away from Seamus, but Eddie didn't want to go. "Math isn't so bad," he told his friends. "Seamus told me you can do all sorts of fun things with it. If I had known that, I would have paid attention sooner."

Melody stopped in the middle of the path and put her hands on her hips. "Well," she said, "you'd better pay attention now because your life may depend on it!"

9

Silenced?

Melody pedaled hard to get far away from Seamus' camper. Eddie, Liza, and Howie raced to catch up with her.

"What were you talking about back there?" Eddie yelled to Melody when his bike finally came neck and neck with hers.

Melody glanced over her shoulder to make sure nobody was following them. She pulled her bike off the path and into the shade of a huge weeping willow tree.

Her friends followed her. They climbed off their bikes and sat in a circle, the drooping tree branches hiding them from sight. Howie's face was red from so much pedaling, and Liza gulped for air.

"What's gotten into you?" Howie asked. "One minute you're looking at a fish tank

and the next minute you're talking nonsense."

"You were riding your bike as if monsters were nipping at your toes," Liza added when she finally caught her breath.

Eddie slapped the ground with his hand. "Why did you drag me away?" he asked. "And what's all that talk about cookies?"

"I'll tell you exactly what's wrong," Melody said. "Seamus Sandborn is a sea serpent!"

Eddie stared at his friend for a full three seconds before he grinned. "And my grandmother is the Loch Ness Monster," he said.

Liza giggled. Eddie's grandmother didn't look a bit like a sea creature.

Melody pointed at Eddie's chest. "Stop making jokes and listen to me. Sea serpents prefer water. They are long and slithery. They're very dangerous — just like your math tutor."

"He can't be a sea serpent," Howie pointed out. "Sea serpents don't juggle water balloons."

"They don't teach math," Liza added.

"And they don't live in campers," Eddie argued.

"They do if they're looking for a place to retire," Melody told her friends. "He told us himself that he wanted a quiet place. I think Seamus is a sea serpent who is planning on living right here next to Viper Pond."

"There are no such things as sea serpents," Liza told Melody. "And even if Seamus was a sea serpent, what difference would it make?"

"What's your favorite school lunch?" Melody asked.

"What does that have to do with sea serpents in Bailey City?" Liza asked.

"Just answer me," Melody said. The three kids thought long and hard.

"Fish sticks," Liza finally said.

“Those are good,” Howie said.

“Especially with lots of ketchup,” Eddie added.

“Well, say good-bye to fish sticks forever,” Melody told them, “because your local sea serpent will gobble up all the fish in Bailey City.”

“You don’t know that Eddie’s tutor likes to eat fish,” Howie argued.

“Think about what’s in his camper,” Melody told them, trying to get them to understand.

The more Liza thought, the bigger her eyes grew. “You mean the tanks full of fish?”

Melody nodded. “An aquarium makes a perfect refrigerator for a sea serpent. Seamus Sandborn’s camper is full of late-night snacks for a sea serpent.”

Eddie shrugged. “Who cares about fish?” he said. “In fact, it’s fine by me if he wants to swallow every fish stick in Bailey City. Then maybe we’ll have pizza more often.”

"And hot dogs," Liza said with a smile.

"Or hamburgers," Howie added, his stomach rumbling.

Melody covered her eyes and shook her head. Then she took a deep breath before looking at her friends again. "No more fish sticks isn't the worst of it. If Seamus really is a sea serpent and he stays in Bailey City, he will stop at nothing to make sure everything is quiet. Very quiet."

"You don't know what you're talking

about," Eddie argued. "A serpent is a snake, and snakes don't have ears. Noise doesn't mean a thing to them."

"That can't be true," Liza said. "Snake charmers use music to train snakes."

"Wait a minute," Howie interrupted. "It isn't the music that charms deadly snakes. It's vibrations caused by the music. If Melody is right and Seamus is a sea serpent, he wouldn't be able to stand the vibrations caused by loud noise."

"YOU ARE MAKING NO SENSE!" Eddie yelled at the top of his lungs.

Melody pointed to Eddie's chest. "You, of all people, should be the most worried," she told Eddie, "because you are famous for making the kind of noise a sea serpent wouldn't like. Seamus wants quiet and he will stop at nothing to get it. Are you ready to be silenced for all time?"

Eddie put his hands on his hips and leaned close to Melody. "Let me get this through your head. I may not like long division, but I am *not* afraid of a silly math tutor."

Melody didn't back away from Eddie. She met him, nose to nose. "Fine, then you won't be afraid to meet back here when the sun goes down."

"Why would we meet here tonight?" Liza interrupted.

"Because," Melody said, looking each of her friends in the eyes. "I'm going to prove to you that Bailey City is facing its greatest threat of all — a sea serpent!"

10

Fishing for Sea Serpents

A few lightning bugs flashed against the evening sky when the kids met at the huge weeping willow. Even though the summer evening was warm, Liza shivered. "Are you sure this is a good idea?" she whispered.

Melody hopped on her bike and nodded. "The Summer Festival is over at the end of this week. We have to do something before then if we plan to save Bailey City. If we don't, Seamus will decide to stay right here in Bailey City instead of moving on with the festival, and we'll all be doomed."

Melody clicked on the light attached to her handlebars. "Are you ready to go fishing for a sea serpent?"

Howie flipped the switch to his light and nodded. "Ready when you are."

Liza sighed and turned on her light. "We might as well get this over with," she said, her voice shaking just a little.

Melody, Liza, and Howie looked at Eddie. "Are you ready?" Melody asked. "Or are you having second thoughts about facing a sea serpent in the dead of night?"

"The only thing that scares me," Eddie said, "is the fact that you're about as smart as one of those lightning bugs." With that, Eddie started pedaling his bicycle down the path that surrounded Swamp Dread.

The four kids silently rode their bikes. The trees next to the swamp blanketed the path in velvety blackness. The only sounds they heard were the buzzing of insects, the pounding of their hearts, and the flutter of bat wings.

As they neared Seamus' camper, Melody

braked to a stop. "We'll go the rest of the way on foot," she whispered, flicking off her light and hiding her bike under another willow tree. Careful not to let her sneakers crunch the broken seashells, she led the way up the path.

They hadn't gone far when they heard a splash. Only this splash didn't sound like it came from Viper Pond. It was too close for that.

"The sea serpent is coming to get us," Liza whimpered.

"Shh," Melody warned. "Follow me."

Melody darted behind an overgrown thicket of trees. They snaked their way closer to the circle of light cast by Seamus' campsite. "That's where the splash came from," Melody said, pointing through the branches.

Howie, Eddie, and Liza gently parted the leaves just enough to peek at Seamus sprawled in the wading pool. "Why would a math tutor be playing in a baby pool?" Eddie asked.

"Because," Melody whispered, "Seamus is soaking in water to make sure his skin doesn't get too scaly."

"I think your brain has grown scales," Eddie said a little too loudly. Seamus sat straight up in the pool.

"Shh," Howie, Melody, and Liza warned at once.

"Now you're starting to hiss like serpents," Eddie grumbled, but he made sure to keep his voice quiet.

Seamus turned his head, first one way, and then another. He dropped one hand outside the pool and spread it flat on the ground.

"What is he doing?" Liza whispered.

Howie answered her with a tightness in his voice that made them all uneasy. "He's feeling the ground for vibrations."

"Just like a sea serpent might do," Melody added softly.

Finally, Seamus stood up from the pool. He didn't bother drying off with a towel. He padded to the camper and disappeared inside. It wasn't long before the door opened and Seamus reappeared. He wore flippers on his feet and carried a big net.

"Oh, my gosh," Liza gulped. "He's coming this way!"

"Run!" Howie yelped.

11

Drastic Action

"Melody's plan is downright crazy," Eddie said. It was the next day and Melody had just told them her idea for getting rid of Seamus.

"We'll end up in big trouble," Liza agreed. "Last night was scary enough. We don't know what might have happened if Seamus had caught us."

"We'll be in bigger trouble if we don't go through with my plan," Melody said.

"Melody is right," Howie added. "We have to make sure Seamus leaves with the rest of the Summer Festival on Saturday. If we wait too long, the carnival will leave town without him and Seamus will settle in for good. We have to try Melody's plan. We'll put it to the test tomorrow during Eddie's tutoring session."

"I don't like the sound of her plan," Liza whimpered.

"I think it sounds like a walk in the park," Eddie said. "No problem at all!"

But Eddie was very wrong.

The kids showed up at Seamus' camper the next day. "Perhapsss you three would like to ssskim ssstones on the pond while Eddie worksss on adding and sssubtracting," Seamus suggested to Liza, Howie, and Melody.

"Of course," Melody said pleasantly. "We'll be no bother at all."

Melody did not mean a single word of what she said. As soon as she had led Howie and Liza around to the back of the camper, they went into action.

"It's time for Operation Noisy," Melody said. "Let's do it!"

Melody, Howie, and even Liza started making noise. Melody clapped. Howie banged two rocks together. Liza snapped her fingers. They clapped and banged and snapped until their hands were tired and

started to tingle. Then the three kids peeked around the corner of the camper. Seamus and Eddie were so busy working with a calculator they didn't seem to notice the noise. In fact, Eddie was so involved, he forgot to be noisy himself.

The next day, Melody, Liza, and Howie tried to be a little louder during Eddie's tutoring session.

Melody bounced a tennis ball off the side of the camper. Howie honked the horn on his bicycle handlebars. Liza tried whistling a tune about a dragon named Puff.

Seamus acted like he hadn't heard a thing, and Eddie seemed to forget about his friends and their noisy plan. He was too interested in learning how to chart the floor of the ocean.

On the third day, Melody faced Howie and Liza. "This calls for drastic action," Melody said. "We only have two more days before that sea serpent takes control of Eddie and the rest of the noisy kids in town. We have to be even louder today."

So Howie, Liza, and Melody made noise — not just a little noise — lots of noise.

Melody cheered.

Howie yelled.

Liza closed her eyes and sang her dragon song so loud her throat started to hurt. She was in the middle of the third verse when she felt a hand grab her shoulder.

Liza screamed. Melody screamed. Howie screamed. All three spun around, ready to battle an angry sea serpent.

What they faced was angry, all right. But it wasn't a sea serpent. It was Eddie's grandmother.

She glared down at the three kids and frowned. "What is the meaning of all this noise?" she asked. "How do you expect poor little Eddie to learn his multiplication facts if you keep distracting him? Now, I want you to be quiet. Very quiet."

Melody gasped when she heard Eddie's grandmother use the exact words that Seamus had used.

"Now skedaddle," Eddie's grandmother told them. "You can see Eddie after his tutoring lesson."

Melody, Liza, and Howie waited for Eddie near the big weeping willow tree. "It looks like Seamus is going to get a quiet city after all," Melody told Eddie when he finally arrived.

Liza sniffed. She was not used to getting in trouble. "I'll never make noise again."

"I'm doomed," Eddie grumbled. "My grandmother is making me be quiet just like Seamus wanted. We might as well give up. We can't battle a sea serpent when my grandmother is on his side."

"We can't quit," Howie argued. "Quitters never succeed. I know what it will take to beat this sea serpent," he said. "And Plan B requires drastic action!"

12

Plan B

"This is too much work," Eddie complained as the kids made posters telling about Plan B.

"Nothing worthwhile is ever easy," Howie admitted. "At least, that's what some famous person once said."

"Can't we just forget all this and have fun at the festival?" Eddie asked. He put his poster down on Liza's kitchen table. His poster read:

> **ATTENTION ALL KIDS!**
>
> Bring your noisemakers for the loudest parade ever!
>
> Meet at the park at 10:00 A.M.

"We can't quit," Liza told him. "Besides, this really isn't hard work. In fact, it's fun."

"Making posters isn't my idea of fun," Eddie grumbled.

"But won't it be cool when all the kids come together for our parade?" Melody asked, putting the cap back on her marker.

"If it works," Liza said.

"We'll find out tomorrow morning," Melody said, "but first we have to get these posters up." The kids walked all around Bailey City putting up posters.

The next morning, they met beside the park entrance to see if any kids would come for the parade. Huey showed up with a drum, and Carrie arrived with a flute. A new girl named Becky had a tambourine. Quite a few other kids had bells, whistles, or horns.

Howie smiled. "I do believe this is going to work."

Eddie crashed his cymbals together. "Let's do it!"

Melody lifted her baton in the air. "Okay, kids, let's march!" she yelled.

Everyone filed into place behind Melody as she cheered in her loudest voice. "March! March!" Liza followed, beating a pot with a wooden spoon. Howie had a homemade tambourine of paper plates and macaroni. Kids from all over Bailey City followed, banging, clanging, and tooting.

BAM! CLANG! TOOT! BAM! CLANG! TOOT!

It was definitely the loudest parade in the history of Bailey City. Eddie's grandmother ran up to the kids and shouted, "Kids! What is all this noise about?"

Melody smiled. "We're having a parade," she explained.

"Oh," Eddie's grandmother said. "Does it have to be so loud?"

"We'll try to play softer," Liza said, but when the kids started playing again, they were as loud as ever.

BAM! CLANG! TOOT! BAM! CLANG! TOOT!

Eddie's grandmother put her hands over her ears as the parade marched past with Melody in the lead. The kids stomped straight to the pool where Seamus was teaching a group to juggle.

BAM! CLANG! TOOT! BAM! CLANG! TOOT!

Seamus gazed at the long and very noisy parade as if he were hypnotized. When Eddie crashed his cymbals together extra hard, Seamus dropped his water balloons, dived into the water, and swam

all the way to the deep end. When he reached the other side, Seamus climbed out of the pool and left the park.

"Do you think it worked?" Liza asked hopefully.

Howie shrugged. "If Seamus really is a sea serpent, the vibrations from the music will drive him far away. He'll think twice about staying in Bailey City!"

Just to make sure, Eddie slammed his cymbals together again as hard as he could.

13

Over

"I can't believe it's over," Melody said the next day as she met Liza, Howie, and Eddie under the school oak tree. "The Summer Festival is gone."

Liza nodded. "We have to wait until next summer to have fun again."

"What are you talking about?" Eddie asked. "It's not over yet. This is still summer and we can still have fun."

"I'm ready," Howie said. The kids jumped on their bikes and raced over to the park. Several kids from their class were playing with Hula-Hoops, and the man with refreshments was trying to get rid of the last of the festival food.

The kids didn't waste any summer time. They joined the group trying to spin Hula-Hoops. Even Liza gave it a whirl.

After about fifteen tries, she was able to make it work — just a little bit.

"All right," Howie cheered. The kids took a break from the Hula-Hoops for a treat of cotton candy.

"This must be the summer of trying," Melody said after swallowing a big hunk of pink cotton candy. "Look what Eddie has tucked in his back pocket."

Eddie licked his fingers and pulled out a math workbook. "Seamus said that to be an astronaut, computer programmer, or a deep-sea diver you have to be good at math, so I figured I would keep trying."

"Does that mean Seamus is still here?" Liza shrieked. "And that you have to be tutored by a sea serpent?"

Eddie grinned. "Nope. My grandmother said I didn't have to go to tutoring anymore as long as I agreed to practice math every day."

"I wonder what happened to Seamus," Howie said.

"He's gone," Eddie told them. "He called

my grandmother and said he couldn't tutor me anymore. He headed out with most of the Summer Festival workers."

"We did it, we did it!" Liza sang and held her cotton candy up in the air.

"We kept trying and we did it!" Melody laughed along with her friends. "We saved Bailey City from a sea serpent!"

"I guess you were right all along," Eddie admitted to Liza. "Quitters never succeed, and I'm going to succeed at juggling!" He grabbed his friends' cotton candy and tried juggling them. One landed with a smack on top of Eddie's head. Another smeared down the front of his chest. One blob of the pink stuff stuck to his chin like a beard and another plopped on his ear.

"I guess we got rid of the sea serpent," Melody said.

"But," Liza said with a laugh, "we ended up with a mess monster!"

TAKE ONE FOR A SPIN!
HULA-HOOP!

Debbie Dadey and Marcia Thornton Jones have fun writing together. When they both worked at an elementary school in Lexington, Kentucky, Debbie was the school librarian and Marcia was a teacher. During their lunch break in the school cafeteria, they came up with the idea of the Bailey School Kids.

Recently Debbie and her family moved to Aurora, Illinois. Marcia and her husband still live in Kentucky, where she continues to teach. How do these authors still write together? They talk on the phone and use computers and fax machines!

Learn more about Debbie and Marcia on their Web site: www.BaileyKids.com